THE DEEP-SEA ADVENTURE SERIES

**JAMES C. COLEMAN**
*Associate Professor of Psychology*
*Director, Clinic School*
*University of California at Los Angeles*

**FRANCES BERRES**
*Assistant Director, Clinic School*
*University of California*
*at Los Angeles*

**FRANK M. HEWETT**
*Instructor in Medical Psychology*
*School of Medicine*
*University of California at Los Angeles*

**WILLIAM S. BRISCOE**
*Professor of Education*
*University of California*
*at Los Angeles*

Dan     Carlos     Andy     Salty

*Illustrations by JOSEPH MANISCALCO*

# Danger
# Below

Bill    Jenkins    Bart    Mr. Duncan

HARR WAGNER PUBLISHING COMPANY • San Francisco

# TABLE OF CONTENTS

## Chapter One

# TWENTY FATHOMS DOWN

Dan moved slowly across the bottom of the sea. He looked out through the glass faceplate of his diving helmet. There before him, like a great gray ghost, was the wreck of the *Western Star*. The cargo ship was lying on the side of an underwater mountain.

Dan saw there would be great danger in trying to salvage the cargo from this wreck. The ship could slip down the mountain and turn over at any time.

The *Western Star* had gone down in twenty fathoms of water, some distance from shore. Now it was lying one hundred and twenty feet below the surface of the sea. The crew had escaped and had been rescued by the Coast Guard. But the *Western Star* was lost. And the important cargo of motors the ship was carrying was lost, too. Dan was trying to find a way to salvage the motors before they were damaged by the sea water.

As Dan moved in for a closer look, several fish swam by him. They swam away quickly as they saw his strange shape moving through the water. The fish seemed afraid of the deep-sea diver in his suit and helmet. His line and air hose and the many air bubbles rising from his helmet were strange to them.

An anchor line came down to the bottom of the sea near Dan. The line came from a boat which floated on the surface of the water over the *Western Star*. This boat was the *Sea Watch*.

On the deck of the *Sea Watch* was an air pump. The air which Dan needed to breathe was pumped down to him under great pressure. The pressure made the air go down through a long hose. Once the air reached Dan, it went into the helmet and diving suit he was wearing. The air inside Dan's suit kept Dan from being squeezed by the great pressure of the water. Also, the air in his suit kept out the cold of the sea. This made it possible for Dan to stay under the water a long time.

Up on the deck of the *Sea Watch* the members of Dan's crew waited while he dived.

Carlos stood watching the pump which sent the air down into Dan's helmet. Carlos was Dan's first mate. He was also a diver. He helped Dan work under the water. With Carlos on the deck of the *Sea Watch* were four other men. Two of them were also crew members of the *Sea Watch*.

2

One of the crew members was a big man called Andy. Andy was the cook on the *Sea Watch*. On Andy's shoulder sat Salty, his parrot.

"Ahoy there, mates! Ahoy there, mates!" said Salty, the parrot.

Andy picked up Salty in his hand.

"How are we ever going to bring up several hundred motors from that ship down there?" said Andy, shaking his head.

Carlos looked up from the air gauge.

"Never mind, Andy," he said. "Dan is down there right now trying to work out a way. You just worry about the cooking."

A man in a gray suit walked over to the air hose. He was Mr. Duncan, the owner of the *Western Star*.

"Dan must find a way to bring up that cargo," said Mr. Duncan. "It is worth a great deal to me."

"Dan will know what to do," said Bill. Bill ran the *Sea Watch* for Dan and took it out from shore to the places where the crew worked. Now he was standing by Dan's air hose and line. He was letting down hose and line to Dan. Bill had a telephone hooked around his head. The telephone cable went down to Dan's helmet. Bill and Dan could talk as Dan worked under the water.

The last man on the deck was Jenkins, the first mate of the *Western Star*. He had a long, pointed face. There were dark shadows under his eyes. Jenkins looked over at Bill.

"What makes you so sure Dan can get to the cargo?" he asked Bill. "Has he ever worked on a salvage mission this big?"

"We have helped bring up several wrecks like the *Western Star*," said Carlos before Bill could answer. "Dan knows what he is doing."

"I hope so," said Jenkins. "Mr. Duncan must get those motors right away. He must get those motors before the water damages them."

Mr. Duncan walked over to Jenkins.

"We just have to salvage that cargo, Jenkins," he said. "You know how important it is to me." He turned back to Carlos. "Are you sure the ship is lying on the side of a mountain down there?" he asked.

"That's right," Carlos answered, closely watching the air pump gauge. "That's what I saw when I went down this morning. I didn't stay down too long but I could see there was danger of the wreck slipping down the mountain at any time."

All at once the men on the deck of the *Sea Watch* heard a voice coming over the telephone. They turned and looked toward Bill. The voice was not clear at first, and the men moved closer to Bill to try and hear better.

"I'm coming around the bow of the wreck, Bill," called Dan over the telephone.

"How cold is it down there?" asked Bill. "Are you going to stay down much longer?"

"I'm not having any trouble with the cold," said Dan. "I'll start up in a few minutes."

"All right, skipper," said Bill. "You have been down a hundred and twenty feet for some time. I'll pull you up slowly. It will take about twenty minutes."

"I'll signal you as soon as I'm ready to come up," said Dan.

Dan slowly moved around the bow of the wrecked ship. He could see there would be only one way to salvage the cargo. They would have to send for two floating docks. Once heavy cables were slipped under the *Western Star* and tied to the floating docks, the ship could be pulled toward shore. With the wreck out of deep water, there would be no trouble bringing up the cargo. But there would be great danger entering the wreck now and trying to bring the motors up to the surface.

Dan was standing on the side of the mountain just below the wreck. As he started to move away from the *Western Star* he saw the gray mud on the bottom of the sea rising high in the water. As he looked out from his faceplate, Dan saw the big ship start to slip. It was moving down on top of him!

## Chapter Two

## THE *SEA DEVIL*

Dan tried to move out of the way of the slipping wreck. But he could not move very quickly. The deep-sea diving gear he was wearing was too heavy. Dan saw the mud rising high in the water. Fish shot by, trying to get out of the way. For a minute, it looked as if there would be no escape. Dan was afraid he was trapped.

But all at once, the wreck stopped slipping down the mountain. It rocked up and down a few times and then came to a full stop not far from Dan. Dan could not see anything around him now because of the mud rising through the water.

"Pull me up, Bill!" he called over the telephone. "I have just had a close call."

Bill started at once to bring in Dan's air hose and line. "Something has gone wrong," he said to the men around him. "Dan just called. He is having trouble down there."

The crew of the *Sea Watch*, Mr. Duncan and Jenkins looked down into the water.

Jenkins was the first one to talk. "It takes a good diver to keep out of trouble in a salvage job like this," he said.

Carlos shot a look at him. "What do you mean by that?" he asked in an angry voice.

Jenkins did not answer him. He turned to Mr. Duncan. "We are not going to save that cargo with a salvage crew that does not know what it is doing," he whispered.

Andy was standing near Mr. Duncan and heard what Jenkins said. He did not say anything, but he thought to himself, "I don't like that Jenkins. He is up to no good, that is for sure."

Bill was pulling Dan up slowly. When Dan was twenty feet below the surface, Bill stopped pulling up the hose and line. Decompression had to start now. Dan would have to wait about twenty minutes at this point before he could be brought to the surface. A diver must go through decompression because of the change in air pressure in his helmet as he is pulled up. When a diver is twenty fathoms below the surface, air must be pumped down to him under great pressure. Under this great pressure, part of the air goes into his blood. The air stays there as long as the diver is working at twenty fathoms. But once a diver is pulled up, the air pressure inside his helmet drops. The bubbles of air that entered the diver's blood under pressure are no longer held there. If a diver is pulled up too quickly, these bubbles come out all at once and can hurt or kill him. This is called "the bends." Pulling a diver up slowly gives the air bubbles a chance to escape a few at a time.

After about twenty minutes, Bill and Carlos helped Dan aboard the *Sea Watch*. They went right to work taking off the heavy helmet. Carlos and Bill worked quickly. Soon they set the helmet down on the deck. All the men waited to hear what Dan had to say.

Dan turned his eyes toward the owner of the *Western Star*.

"Well, Dan," said Mr. Duncan, "what did you find? How soon can we get to the cargo?"

Dan had started to take off his heavy diving suit. He took a deep breath before he answered.

"The wreck is slipping down the mountain. There is no way to bring up the cargo right now. We must wait until we get the *Western Star* held in place with cables or pull it in closer to shore. We will need two floating docks."

"But that may take days!" cried Mr. Duncan. "Are you sure there is no other way?"

"That is the only way," answered Dan. "No diver would take a chance diving inside that wreck now. It could turn over and trap him at any time."

Carlos and Bill helped Dan take off his diving suit. Then Dan went inside the *Sea Watch*.

Jenkins moved close to Mr. Duncan. "It will be a long time until the floating docks can be brought out," he said. "The cargo will be damaged."

"I know," said Mr. Duncan. "If only there were another way."

"Ship ahoy! Ship ahoy!" cried Salty. The parrot flew off Andy's shoulder and on to the side of the boat.

Bill and Carlos looked out over the water. In the distance they saw a boat coming toward them. The two men held their hands over their eyes to get a better look. They could see *Sea Devil* on the boat's bow.

"The *Sea Devil*?" said Carlos. "I have never seen that boat before."

"I have," said Jenkins, coming over to the side. He waved to the men aboard the *Sea Devil*. Then he looked at Mr. Duncan and said, "I sent for the *Sea Devil* last night. I sent out a message for it over your boat's radio." Mr. Duncan's boat was anchored not far from the *Sea Watch*. This boat had brought Mr. Duncan and Jenkins out to the wreck.

"What do you mean, Jenkins?" asked Mr. Duncan in surprise.

11

"Well, I didn't tell you before," answered Jenkins, "but I was afraid the crew of the *Sea Watch* would not be able to help us."

"Dan and his men were to have first chance at this salvage mission," said Mr. Duncan, shaking his head. "You had no right to bring out another ship on your own."

"Listen, Mr. Duncan," said Jenkins. "You know I want to help you in any way I can. I asked to come along just so I could be of help when you needed me."

"I know, Jenkins," said Mr. Duncan. "But Dan has said. . . ."

Jenkins moved close to Mr. Duncan. "These men don't know what they are doing," he whispered. "If you listen to them, your cargo will be gone for good."

The *Sea Devil* moved closer to the *Sea Watch* and dropped anchor. A small boat was put into the water and a man rowed over to the *Sea Watch*.

"Ahoy, Jenkins," the man called as he rowed his boat along the side of the *Sea Watch*.

"Bart!" Jenkins called back. "You and your crew got here just in time."

In a few minutes Bart came aboard the *Sea Watch*. He shook Jenkins' hand and looked around at the other men on deck.

12

"When do we go to work?" he asked.

Just then Dan came outside. Jenkins turned to him and pointed at Bart.

"Bart is the owner of the *Sea Devil*. He and his crew have come to take a look at the *Western Star*," he said. "I don't think they will be afraid to go after the cargo in the holds."

Carlos had not said anything up to this time. But now he could no longer keep still.

"We will take care of this salvage mission," he said to Bart. "You can clear out of here fast."

Jenkins looked at Mr. Duncan. "All I ask is that Bart have a chance to look at the wreck. He knows all about salvage jobs."

Mr. Duncan thought for a minute. "Well, I asked Dan first to look over the job," he said slowly. "But it would not hurt to let another diver go down and see what he thinks."

Carlos began to move toward Jenkins and Bart. His hands were up ready for a fight. But Dan held him back.

"Wait a minute, Carlos," Dan said. "If Mr. Duncan wants another diver to look at the *Western Star*, it is all right with me."

Jenkins moved quickly toward the side of the boat.

"Come on, Mr. Duncan," he said. "Let's go over to the *Sea Devil*."

Mr. Duncan turned to Dan. "You still have first chance for the job, Dan," he said. "But if we can get those motors up here before they are damaged, I want to do it."

Dan walked over to the side of the *Sea Watch* where Bart was getting into his small boat.

"If you dive," Dan said to Bart, "be sure and keep away from the wreck. The ship is slipping and could turn over any time. I was almost trapped down there."

"Don't listen to him," said Jenkins. "He is afraid to take a chance."

Bart rowed away in his small boat. Mr. Duncan and Jenkins followed him in their small boat which had been tied up by the *Sea Watch*.

"Why did you let them get away with that, Dan?" asked Carlos, once they had left.

"Take it easy, Carlos," said Dan. "Bart will soon see the danger down there. Don't forget, Mr. Duncan just said we still have first chance for the job."

The men on the *Sea Watch* could see Bart getting ready for his dive. Soon he was let down into the sea.

Time went on and he was not pulled up. All at once, one of the men on the *Sea Devil* rowed very fast over to the *Sea Watch*. He was out of breath as he came aboard. He turned to Dan.

"Bart has been down too long," he said. "The telephone is not working so we can't talk to him. It is possible he is in trouble. Our other diver is not with us. Will you go down and see what is wrong?"

Carlos moved in. "Dan didn't ask Bart to dive," he said. "Why should. . . ."

Dan stopped him. "Get my gear ready," he said. "I'll go down and see if Bart is in danger."

Bill and Carlos helped Dan change into his diving suit and helmet. Soon he was on his way to the bottom.

Once Dan was down, he looked for Bart's air hose and line. He did not have to look long. Bart's air hose and line were going into the *Western Star*. Bart had gone inside the wreck!

Dan stopped for a minute and thought. It was very possible that Bart was in trouble. There was also a chance that the wreck would start slipping again. What should he do?

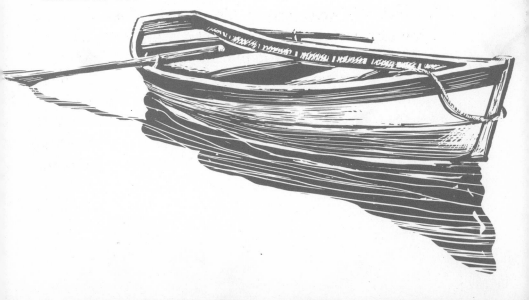

*Chapter Three*

# KNIFE ATTACK!

Dan knew he must find out if Bart needed help. He headed at once for the deck of the *Western Star*. Slowly he walked up on the wreck and into a hold, following Bart's air hose and line. Dan had brought an underwater light with him. He turned it on as he entered the dark ship. He saw that Bart's line and hose went deep inside the *Western Star*. Dan went deeper and deeper into the ship after them.

As Dan moved slowly through the wreck, thoughts about Bart went through his mind. Dan had not liked the way Jenkins had brought this other diver into the salvage job. Now he didn't like the risk this strange diver was taking. Why would any diver enter a wreck after he had been told it was in danger of slipping?

Dan moved his light around him as he went on. It was cold and dark inside the wreck. Dan moved on and on through the damaged ship. He could see hundreds of cases of motors on all sides of the hold.

As he moved through the wreck, Dan saw a light some distance ahead. "Bart must be up there," Dan thought. At last he reached the door that opened into the hold where the light came from. As he entered the hold, Dan saw a strange thing. The water was only a few feet deep. He found himself standing in air!

Dan knew that he must be in an air lock. When the *Western Star* had gone down, most of the air inside it had escaped through portholes and other openings out into the sea. But in this part of the ship, the air had been trapped. It had not escaped out into the sea.

Dan saw that the light was coming from behind several cases of motors. He moved slowly toward the light. Then he saw Bart. The diver from the *Sea Devil* had his back to Dan and was trying to open one of the cases. The case had 749 on the outside. Bart held a hammer in his hand. Dan heard the sound of the hammer as it hit the case over and over again.

All at once Bart stopped hammering. Something made him turn around. When he saw Dan standing behind him, Bart moved away from the case. He started toward Dan.

Seeing Dan in the hold upset Bart. There was an angry look on his face, and he held the hammer up high. It looked as if he might try to hit Dan with it. He moved slowly toward Dan, holding the hammer before him!

Dan held up his light to get a better look at Bart. He reached for the knife which was hooked at his side. He did not know what this strange diver would do. But if Bart started to attack, Dan was ready to fight back.

All at once the ship began slipping. Bart fell back into the water in the bottom of the air lock. Dan kept himself from going down by holding tightly to a case. The ship was slipping more and more. Dan started moving out of the hold. He fell first one way, then another, as the wreck slipped slowly down the underwater mountain. Dan knew there was not much time to escape!

The inside of the *Western Star* was dark. Dan had trouble seeing how to get out. Slowly he squeezed through the cases and made his way to the deck. The sea was black with mud rising up through the water. Dan moved away from the wreck as quickly as he could. By this time the ship had stopped slipping.

Dan turned to look back at the wreck. But just then something grabbed him. It was Bart. The other diver had escaped from the *Western Star* with Dan.

Bart grabbed Dan's shoulder and reached for the knife Dan was carrying at his side. Dan's hand came down on Bart's arm and squeezed tightly. Then Dan hit Bart and knocked him down. As Bart fell, the mud started rising up around him. But Bart was not down long. He came at Dan and tried to pull him down. The two divers were soon covered with mud. All at once Dan backed into a rock and fell over it. Before he could get up, Bart was on top of him. Bart grabbed Dan's knife and quickly pulled away.

As Dan got up to go after Bart, he saw a very strange thing. Bart held Dan's knife in his hand. As Dan moved toward him, Bart began to cut into his own diving suit. As soon as the knife cut through the suit, the air began to escape. Bubbles shot up through the water.

Dan had never seen anything like this! Once a diver's suit is cut, the air pressure around him goes down. If the air pressure inside his suit goes down too fast, a diver may be squeezed by the great pressure of the water around him. If the pressure of the water hits him all at once, the diver may be killed. Why should Bart do a thing like that?

As soon as Bart had cut his own suit, he dropped the knife. Then he pulled fast on his line. He pulled four times, over and over. This was the signal that he was in trouble. When a diver does not have a telephone, or if the one he has is not working, he can signal by pulling on his line. The man holding the line on the deck of the *Sea Devil* got Bart's signal. At once he started pulling Bart up fast through the water.

Dan called over the telephone to Bill.

"Something very strange has taken place," he said. "Start pulling me up right away."

Dan was pulled up slowly. As he neared the surface, he was stopped from time to time so that decompression could take place. As Dan waited, he thought about Bart. He thought about what he had seen deep inside the wreck of the *Western Star*. Dan also thought about the way Bart had attacked him and then cut his own suit.

It was not long before Dan was pulled over the side of the *Sea Watch*. He wanted to find out what had gone on after Bart was pulled up. As Carlos and Bill took off his diving helmet, Dan got a good look at them. They both had a look of worry on their faces.

"What about Bart, Carlos?" Dan asked.

"He is over there on the *Sea Devil*," Carlos said slowly. "He has just been put into the decompression chamber."

"What took place down there, skipper?" asked Bill. "Do you know what Bart's story is?"

Dan looked at Bill.

"What has Bart told the men on his ship?" he asked.

Carlos did not give Bill a chance to answer. "One of his men just came over and told us," he said. "Bart told Mr. Duncan you pulled a knife on him. He said you tried to kill him!"

24

*Chapter Four*

## BART'S STORY

A look of surprise came across Dan's face.

"Bart said what?" he asked.

"We told that crew member Bart was wrong," said Bill. "We knew he was wrong, skipper."

"What *did* go on down there?" asked Carlos. "How did Bart's suit get cut?"

"Help me get out of this gear," said Dan. "I have a feeling we are in for trouble."

Carlos and Bill helped Dan take off the diving suit. As they worked, Dan told them about finding Bart trying to open one of the motor cases in the hold. He also told them how Bart had cut his own suit with Dan's knife.

Andy came out on deck and listened to what Dan said.

"I would like to take care of Bart," said Andy, shaking his head. "I have a cooking knife or two that will cut up his suit for him."

"He wanted to get you into trouble, Dan," said Bill.

"And I think I know why," said Dan. "This is a way for Bart to get the salvage mission away from us."

"I have been thinking about that," said Carlos. "That must be what he is trying to do. It also sounds as if he is after something inside that hold he doesn't want us to know about."

Carlos walked to the side of the *Sea Watch* and looked at the *Sea Devil*. "Look at them," he said. "They are all standing around the decompression chamber watching Bart. He has them all worrying about him."

The crew of the *Sea Devil* had pulled Bart up fast to save him. But decompression had not taken place. Bart had not been brought up slowly enough to let the air bubbles in his blood escape a few at a time. There was a chance he might get the bends. That was why he had been put inside the decompression chamber.

A pump had been turned on and was pumping air under pressure into the chamber. The air inside the chamber was now at the same pressure it had been while Bart was diving. A crew member stood by watching the air gauge. Slowly he brought down the air pressure inside the decompression chamber. In this way the air bubbles in Bart's blood could escape slowly. He would not get the bends.

26

Two of the men waiting for Bart to come out of the decompression chamber were Mr. Duncan and Jenkins.

"Bart's story can't be right," said Mr. Duncan. "I don't think Dan would ever try to kill any one." The owner of the *Western Star* seemed very upset.

Jenkins put his hand on Mr. Duncan's arm.

"I am just as surprised as you are, Mr. Duncan," he said, with a stern look on his face. Then he looked toward the *Sea Watch*. "Don't forget, some men will do anything to keep a salvage job as big as this one."

Mr. Duncan pulled away from Jenkins. "But I know Dan," he said. "This is not like him at all."

On the deck of the *Sea Watch*, the crew saw Jenkins and Mr. Duncan looking over at them.

"Something strange is going on," said Dan. "I want to talk to Mr. Duncan. He has to hear the real story right away."

Carlos and Dan put a small boat down into the water. They got into it and rowed over to the *Sea Devil*. As Dan and Carlos neared the other ship, they could see Bart's crew waiting for them. Dan could tell from the angry looks on their faces that they were all against him.

"Get away from here before you get hurt," one of the men called in an angry voice.

"Don't come any closer," another one said. "We don't want any killers on this ship."

Dan and Carlos rowed up next to the *Sea Devil*. Dan started to go aboard. But before he could get on deck, two of the crew attacked him. Dan fell back into the small boat. Blood ran from a cut on his head.

Carlos jumped aboard the *Sea Devil*, ready to fight. But the men were waiting for him, too. Two men grabbed Carlos and held his arms tightly. Another started to hit him in the face.

"Stop! Stop!" cried Mr. Duncan coming up behind them. "This fighting has gone far enough!"

Jenkins ran up and pulled the crew members away from Carlos. "You are out of your mind to come over here after what Dan did to Bart," he said.

"Listen here," called Dan from the small boat. "Give me a chance to tell my side of the story. Bart is wrong. I never pulled my knife on him. Bart took my knife and cut his own suit."

"What?" cried Jenkins. "Bart cut his own suit? Listen to that, men. Bart cut his own suit!"

The crew members laughed. "That's a good one," said one of the men.

"Don't ever think we will go for that story," said Jenkins. "You had better clear out of here fast."

"Mr. Duncan," called Dan, "what I am telling you is right. Bart attacked me and then used my knife to cut his own suit. It is part of a plan to get the salvage job for himself."

Jenkins turned to Mr. Duncan. "Did you hear that, Mr. Duncan?" he asked. "Are you going to take a chance with a diver like that? He is a killer. He tried to kill a man to keep a salvage job. There is no telling what more he will do before he is through."

Mr. Duncan looked down at Dan. "Your story sounds strange, Dan," he said. "I don't like to think you tried to kill Bart, but. . . ."

"But he did!" cried Jenkins. "You don't want a killer working for you. We must radio the Coast Guard and turn him in."

"I don't know what to say," began Mr. Duncan.

"I do," said Jenkins. "Clear out, Dan, before we take the Coast Guard's job into our own hands." Jenkins looked at Mr. Duncan. "You want Bart and the crew of the *Sea Devil* to salvage the *Western Star*, don't you?" he asked.

Mr. Duncan thought for a minute. "Yes, that's right," he said slowly. "You are through, Dan. This is Bart's job now."

"You will find out how wrong you are, Mr. Duncan," said Dan. "There will be trouble ahead if you listen to Jenkins and Bart."

"Clear out of here fast," called one of the crew members.

Dan and Carlos rowed back to the *Sea Watch*. Andy and Bill were waiting for them. They had seen the fight on the *Sea Devil*.

"What are we going to do, skipper?" asked Bill.

"You can't let Bart get away with this," cried Carlos. "I would like to go back and fight all that crew."

"Take it easy, Carlos," said Dan. "We will find a way to show Mr. Duncan that Bart is wrong. And we won't have to fight to do it."

The crew of the *Sea Watch* sat down and talked over what had gone on. They had much to worry about. What could be done to clear Dan?

The sun was going down and it began to get dark. The ships anchored over the wreck stood out like shadows against the deep blue sky. This had been a strange start for the salvage of the *Western Star*.

*Chapter Five*

# TRAPPED!

The surface of the water glistened like glass in the morning sun. Andy was the first crew member out on the deck of the *Sea Watch*. He walked across the deck with Salty, the parrot, on his shoulder.

"This will be a great day for diving," said Andy, looking up at the blue sky. "But from the looks of things Carlos and Dan won't be going down."

"Ship ahoy!" said Salty. "Ship ahoy!"

Andy looked over at the *Sea Devil*, which was still anchored not far away. There were no men on the deck.

"That boat really brought trouble with it," he thought.

As Andy stood looking at the *Sea Devil*, Salty flew off his shoulder. The parrot flew up in the air and headed for the other boat.

"Salty! Salty!" cried Andy. "Come back here."

But Salty did not mind Andy. The parrot flew across the water to the deck of the *Sea Devil*.

"Salty!" called Andy. "Keep away from there. Come back! Come back!"

But Andy's calling did not do any good. Salty stayed on the *Sea Devil*. Andy thought for a minute. Then he moved fast. He jumped into the small boat which was tied to the *Sea Watch* and pulled away the line. Then Andy took hold of the two oars and started to row. The oars splashed up and down in the water. Andy had never done much rowing before and he was having trouble.

As the small boat splashed away from the *Sea Watch*, Carlos and Bill looked out of one of the portholes. They saw their cook heading for the *Sea Devil*.

"Andy!" called Carlos. "Where do you think you're going all alone?"

Andy did not answer. He just kept rowing toward the *Sea Devil*.

"Come back here, Andy!" called Bill. "Don't go near that boat."

But Andy was not listening. Closer and closer he rowed to the *Sea Devil*. He looked over his shoulder at Salty up on the deck.

By now two crew members had come out on the deck of the *Sea Devil*. They saw Andy nearing the boat.

"It's another one of the crew of the *Sea Watch*," said one of the men. "If he is looking for trouble, he has come to the right place."

34

Andy was almost next to the *Sea Devil*. He could hear what the man said.

"I'm only after my parrot," he called over his shoulder.

The small boat rocked in the water as the oars splashed up and down. Several more men came out on deck. One of them was Jenkins. He walked to the side of the boat and watched Andy row up next to the bow.

"It's the cook from the *Sea Watch*," he called back to Bart, who was just coming outside. Bart had been taken out of the decompression chamber the night before and was all right now.

"What does he want?" asked Bart, walking over to Jenkins.

"Come on, Salty. Come down here," called Andy as the small boat rocked in the water. But Salty flew away.

"So that's it!" said Jenkins, seeing Salty for the first time. "He has come after that parrot!"

"Here Salty! Here Salty!" called Andy.

"I'll take care of your parrot for you," said Jenkins in a stern voice. He started moving slowly toward Salty.

"Forget about that parrot, Jenkins," said Bart. "I want to get suited up right away for another dive."

"This won't take long," said Jenkins. "You should be glad for a chance to get back at the men who almost killed you."

Bart turned away. "Have it your own way, Jenkins," he said. "But I'm going to get ready." He waved to one of his crew members. "Give me a hand here, will you?"

Jenkins moved closer and closer to Salty. He was just about to grab the parrot when Salty flew up on a high cable.

"Salty! Salty!" cried Andy, keeping the small boat next to the *Sea Devil*.

Dan, Carlos and Bill had come out on the deck of the *Sea Watch*. They stood together watching what was going on.

"That parrot!" said Carlos. "This time he is in real trouble. I have told Andy he should keep Salty tied up."

"I hope Andy doesn't try to go aboard the *Sea Devil* after Salty," said Dan. "He may get hurt. Those men are just waiting to start something again."

Jenkins was not going to give up. He stood up on the side of the *Sea Devil* and reached out toward the cable after Salty. The parrot slowly moved up the cable which went out over the water. Jenkins reached up after him. Jenkins' hands were coming closer and closer.

"Salty, get away! Get away!" called Andy.

Jenkins was right behind Salty now. He made one fast move and grabbed for the parrot. Just as he had his hands on Salty, the parrot shot up in the sky. Jenkins fell head first off the boat! There was a big splash as he hit the water. Salty flew to the small boat and to Andy's shoulder. Andy started rowing as fast as possible for the *Sea Watch*.

Jenkins came to the surface of the water.

"I'll get you for this," he called in an angry voice. "You wait and see!"

By this time, Andy was some distance away from the *Sea Devil*. He kept the oars moving very fast. Water splashed up on all sides, but Andy was moving the boat through the water.

Jenkins was helped aboard Bart's ship. The crew members could not keep from laughing at what they had seen. Jenkins stood looking after Andy. He hit the side of the ship with his hand. He was very angry.

On the deck of the *Sea Watch*, Carlos and Bill were laughing, too.

"Did you see the way Jenkins fell into the water?" Carlos laughed. "He really must have been surprised."

"Good for Salty," said Bill. "He showed Jenkins a thing or two."

Andy rowed up next to the *Sea Watch*.

"I'll get you for this!" said Salty from Andy's shoulder. "I'll get you for this!"

Dan laughed along with the others.

"That's what Jenkins said when he came up out of the water," said Andy, as the men helped him from the small boat. The boat was tied up and the men sat on the deck to talk.

"I have to hand it to you, Andy," said Carlos when he stopped laughing. "You were not afraid to go over there after Salty."

Andy did not answer. He looked at the parrot on his shoulder. "You stay on the *Sea Watch* after this, Salty," he said. Then he turned to Dan. "Bart is going to dive this morning. They are helping him get ready now."

All the smiles left the faces of the crew. They turned and looked at the *Sea Devil*. A diver was just going over the side and down into the clear blue water. His diving helmet glistened in the sun.

"There goes Bart," said Carlos. He looked over at Mr. Duncan's boat which was lying near the *Sea Devil*. A small boat was just pulling away from it. It was headed for Bart's boat.

"Mr. Duncan is on his way to the *Sea Devil*," said Bill. "We have to find some way to clear Dan with him."

Dan got up and walked to the side of the *Sea Watch*. He looked down into the water. "I really would like to see what Bart does once he gets to the wreck," he said. "I have a feeling he will enter the hold where I found him before."

Carlos came over next to him. "It sounds as if Bart is up to something," he said. "What do you think he's trying to get out of the wreck?"

"I don't know," answered Dan. "But I have been thinking about diving down and trying to find out."

"But, skipper," said Bill, "there is no telling what Bart may do if you dive after him."

Andy pointed over to the men on the *Sea Devil.* "And there is no telling what they might do if they saw you go down."

"It may be the only way," said Dan. "I'll take the chance."

Carlos was deep in thought. "Wait, Dan," he said. "Let me go down. I'll put on the scuba gear and dive after Bart. That way no one will see me."

Dan thought for a minute. "You know the danger you will face down there. Bart may attack you. Also, there is a chance the wreck will start slipping again."

"I'll be all right, Dan," said Carlos. "I will be able to move better through the water than Bart."

The men helped Carlos get into the scuba gear. Soon he was wearing a black rubber suit. He put flippers on his feet and hooked a glass mask tightly over his face. Two air tanks tied together went on his back. An air hose went from the tanks into a breathing tube which Carlos would hold in his mouth. With this gear, Carlos could move like a fish under the water. No air hose or line from the deck of the *Sea Watch* was needed.

Dan and Bill looked at the gauge on the air tanks.

"Both tanks are full," said Dan. "Don't stay down long and try not to let Bart know you are there."

"Thanks, Dan. I'll be all right," said Carlos, picking up his underwater light. He put the breathing tube in his mouth and walked to the stern of the *Sea Watch*. From there he could not be seen by the men on the *Sea Devil*. No one on the other ship would know of the secret dive.

Carlos swam down toward the wreck. The flippers helped him move fast. Soon Carlos came across Bart's air hose and line. He saw that they entered the wreck. Carlos followed the air hose and line inside the wreck. He turned on his underwater light and slowly made his way through the cargo ship. As Carlos neared the air lock, he turned off his light and hoped Bart would not see him. Slowly Carlos came up through the water into the air lock and looked around. There, up ahead, was Bart at work. He had just opened Case 749 and was pulling back the sides. Inside the case was a motor.

Bart reached into the motor and brought out a small black case. Carlos watched him closely.

"There must be something in that small black case worth a great deal," thought Carlos. "Bart has risked his life to get it."

Bart did not open the small case but started at once

42

to go. As he turned, Bart saw Carlos in the water. Bart stopped and waited. Carlos waited, too.

"If I can just get that black case," thought Carlos.

Carlos moved slowly toward Bart. He knew he would have to fight for that black case. Carlos hoped to knock Bart over in the water. The deep-sea diving gear Bart was wearing was very heavy. Once Bart was down it would not be easy for him to get up again.

Bart saw Carlos coming toward him. He reached down for the knife at his side. Just then the wreck started slipping and both divers fell. As the ship rocked, the water in the air lock splashed up on the sides of the hold. The black case flew from Bart's hand and fell into the water. Carlos dived down and grabbed it before Bart could stand up.

The wreck was still slipping when Carlos started out of the hold. He held on to the black case and swam fast. At last Carlos was in open water.

Deep inside the *Western Star*, Bart had not moved from the hold. The wreck had stopped slipping and all was still. Bart took the faceplate from his helmet. His face was lined with worry. Bart knew his air hose and line had been cut when the wreck slipped. He held up his underwater light and looked through the gray shadows in the hold. He was trapped alone, twenty fathoms under the sea, with only the air in the air lock to breathe!

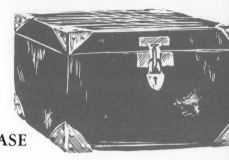

*Chapter Six*

# THE BLACK CASE

Carlos swam for the *Sea Watch*. He followed the anchor line up toward the surface. From time to time he stopped so that decompression could take place. Both helmet and scuba divers must get used to the change in air pressure as they come up. As he swam, Carlos held the black case tightly in one hand. When at last he reached the surface, he found Dan, Bill and Andy waiting for him.

"Carlos!" said Dan, helping him aboard. "Are you all right?"

Carlos took the breathing tube from his mouth. "I'm all right," he answered. He held up the case. "This is what Bart was after. I got it away from him when the wreck started slipping."

In a minute Carlos was standing on the deck of the *Sea Watch*. The water ran off his black rubber suit. Bill helped him take off the face mask and air tanks. All the men were looking at the black case.

Carlos set the case down on the deck. It was locked. As the men looked at it closely, Carlos told them how he had taken it from Bart.

Dan turned and looked over at the *Sea Devil.* "Bart has not been brought up," he said.

"He may never be brought up," said Carlos slowly. "As I left, I didn't see if he made it out or not. But I do know that the wreck slipped a long way. His air hose and line could have been cut."

"Then Bart may be trapped down there—a hundred and twenty feet below the surface," said Dan, shaking his head.

"What's inside the case?" asked Andy after a minute.

"We would all like to know that," answered Dan. "But we do know it was worth enough for Bart to risk his life."

"He may have lost his life, too," said Carlos. "The wreck is not in good shape." He picked up the black case and looked at the lock on the top. "What do you say we try and open it, Dan?"

"No, I think we had better let Mr. Duncan do that," came the answer. "The only way to clear things up is to turn it over to him right away."

"Look!" said Andy, pointing toward the *Sea Devil.* "You won't have to wait any longer."

The crew of the *Sea Watch* saw two men starting over in a small boat.

"Well, what do you know," said Bill. "Here come Jenkins and Mr. Duncan. "Look, there seems to be something important going on over on the deck of the *Sea Devil*."

The crew of Bart's boat could be seen looking over the side of the ship. They were looking at Bart's air hose and line. The men seemed to be very upset.

In a few minutes the small boat rowed up next to the *Sea Watch*. Mr. Duncan had a look of worry on his face.

"There has been real trouble, Dan," he said, once he was aboard. "Bart is lost."

Carlos stood so that the small black case was behind him on the deck. It could not be seen by the two men who had just come aboard. Jenkins did not seem to have much to say. He stood next to Mr. Duncan and kept his head bowed.

"Ahoy!" said Salty. "Ahoy!"

Jenkins shot an angry look at the parrot and then looked down again.

"What do you mean, Bart's lost?" asked Dan.

"Both his air hose and line have been cut," said Mr. Duncan. "The wreck must have slipped again and cut the lines."

"Was Bart inside the wreck again?" asked Dan, as if he did not know what had gone on.

"No, he was not inside the wreck," said Jenkins in

an angry voice. "Don't you think for a minute that story of yours will hold up just because Bart is gone. The Coast Guard will. . . ."

"Keep still, Jenkins," said Mr. Duncan. "We did not come over for another fight. There has been enough of that. I came over to ask Dan if he would dive down and see if we can save Bart some way."

Carlos moved toward Mr. Duncan. "Why should Dan risk his life for Bart?" he said. "There is great danger in diving down there."

Jenkins pulled Mr. Duncan back. "I told you it would be no use," he said. "These men will be glad if Bart is killed."

"Don't mind Jenkins," said Mr. Duncan. "Dan, I know you will help us."

"If I thought for a minute there was any way to rescue Bart, I would dive," said Dan. "But when a man's air hose has been cut, he can't last long."

Dan walked over to Mr. Duncan. "We know Bart was inside the wreck again," he said. "Carlos found him there trying to take this out of the hold." As he said this, Dan pointed behind Carlos to the small black case.

Jenkins started toward the case with a surprised look on his face.

"Where did you. . ." he said. Then he stopped and pulled back. "What's that?" he asked.

Dan picked up the case and set it before Mr. Duncan. "This is what Bart was after the day I found him inside the wreck," he said. Then he told the story of Carlos and Bart.

"Bart was not able to get the small black case on his first dive because the wreck started slipping," Dan went on. "But this morning Carlos found him at work in the same place."

Mr. Duncan picked up the case. He shook it and then tried to open the lock. Andy handed Mr. Duncan a hammer. It was only a small lock, and after Mr. Duncan hit it a few times the case came open. The top of the case was pulled back and the men were able to see what was inside.

"Diamonds!" cried Carlos. "Look at all those diamonds!"

The black case was full of diamonds of all shapes. Some were small, but most of them were very big. The diamonds glistened in the sun. It almost hurt the men's eyes to look at them.

"Think what these are worth," said Bill. "It's easy to see now why Bart was willing to risk his life."

Mr. Duncan closed the cover over the glistening diamonds. He stood up and looked at the men around him. "There is only one way these diamonds could have been placed aboard the *Western Star*. This is the work of smugglers."

Jenkins, who had not said very much before, now came up to Mr. Duncan. "Then Bart was really a diamond smuggler!" he said. "And to think that we all were taken in by him."

Dan looked at Jenkins. "We *all* were not taken in by him," he said. "We tried to tell you there was something strange. . . ."

Before Dan was through, Jenkins moved close to him. He put his hand on Dan's shoulder and smiled.

"Dan," he said, "what must you think of me? All the time I was trying to help a diamond smuggler. And I called you a killer. How can I ever make up for what I have done to you and your crew?"

Dan pulled away. He still did not like Jenkins. "It looks as if Bart's days as a diamond smuggler are over," he said.

"We must radio the Coast Guard and get these diamonds to them right away," said Mr. Duncan. "I was wrong, too, Dan. I feel very upset about what I said and did."

"What about Bart?" Bill asked Dan. "Are you going to dive after him?"

Before Dan could answer, Jenkins cried out, "I should hope not! I would not want Dan to risk his life for that smuggler. Bart had this coming to him."

"Jenkins has been wrong all the time," said Mr. Duncan. "But I really think he is right now. There is no longer a chance of helping Bart. Also, that wreck may start slipping again. I'm going back to my ship and radio the Coast Guard. If you are still willing to help us, Dan, I'll be back to talk over salvage plans with you."

"That's right, we'll be back," smiled Jenkins. "From now on the job is in Dan's hands."

As Mr. Duncan started to get into the small boat, he handed the black case full of diamonds to Jenkins. "Guard this for me," he said. "Lock them up when we get back to the boat."

"Yes, Mr. Duncan," said Jenkins. "I'll be glad to take care of them for you." He smiled and waved to the crew of the *Sea Watch*. "See you soon," he called as he started rowing away.

Andy shook his head. "I really don't like that Jenkins," he said. "There is something about him that. . . ."

"I think that goes for all of us, Andy," said Dan. "But let's move fast. We don't have much time. Help me into the scuba gear, Carlos."

"What for?" asked Carlos.

"I'm going down," said Dan. "There is a small chance Bart is still in the air lock. If he is, I may be able to save him."

"But why risk your life, skipper?" asked Bill. "There is no telling what shape the wreck is in now."

"Just the same, it's something I have to do," said

54

Dan, picking up the black rubber suit, face mask and two flippers. "I know Bart was working against us. But if there is any chance to save another diver, I have to take it."

The men worked fast to get Dan ready. Just before he dived, he asked for another rubber suit, flippers and a glass face mask. Then Dan slipped over the stern of the *Sea Watch* and headed down under the sea on his strange rescue mission.

*Chapter Seven*

## BART'S SECRET

As Dan swam deeper and deeper into the sea, he knew there was not much hope for Bart. The air in the air lock might have escaped when the wreck slipped, and the hold could be full of water. But he had to find out. Dan thought it was strange that he was on his way again to try and rescue a man who had been so much trouble. But Dan also knew that any diver would have done the same thing.

Dan found the wreck still lying on the side of the underwater mountain. He could tell it had slipped a great distance after his dive the day before. Then Dan saw something that brought a look of worry to his face. Dan saw air bubbles rising from the *Western Star*. This could mean only one thing. Some of the air that had been trapped inside the ship was escaping.

Dan entered the wreck at once. He turned on his underwater light and swam for the hold deep inside. He soon saw the cut part of Bart's air hose and line floating ahead of him in the water. He knew the diver from the *Sea Devil* had never made it out of the wreck. As Dan swam into the hold, he was surprised to see the air lock still there. He pointed the light around the hold and found Bart. The other diver was standing in the water, his helmet still in place. Dan could see that Bart had taken off his faceplate.

Dan took the breathing tube out of his mouth and called out, "Bart, I have come to help you. Are you all right?"

Bart moved toward Dan. "You mean you came to rescue me?" he said. "I had just about lost all hope."

"I have brought a rubber suit for you to wear," said Dan. "I'll help you take off that helmet and change diving suits. We both can use my breathing tube to get back to the surface."

"Thanks, Dan," said Bart.

Dan looked around the hold. "The air is escaping now," he said. "We must move fast." He started taking off Bart's heavy helmet.

"The black case," said Bart. "Did Jenkins get the diamonds?"

"Yes," answered Dan while he worked. "The diamonds were turned over to Mr. Duncan."

By now Bart's helmet was almost off. Dan turned it and pulled it up over Bart's head. He started helping Bart out of the deep-sea diving gear.

"Listen, Dan," said Bart. "You have to listen to this. It won't take long. I'll change into the rubber suit while we talk."

"There is no need to say anything," said Dan. "The most important job is to get out as fast as we can."

"I know you think I must be working with the diamond smugglers," said Bart. "But you are wrong. I have been trying to catch the diamond smugglers."

Dan looked up in surprise. "Trying to *catch* the smugglers?" he asked.

"That's right," Bart went on. "I am a secret agent. I have been working on this diamond case for some time. And I was just about to catch the head of the smugglers when I was trapped down here."

"That's some story!" Dan said after a time. He was very surprised by what Bart was saying. Was this man lying to him at a time like this? Or was he a real secret agent?

"I am telling you this, Dan, because I need your help," said Bart. "No one on my boat knows I am an agent. My working as a diver and owner of the *Sea Devil* is all part of a plan to trap the smugglers. You must not tell any one about me. But if something goes wrong and I can't get out of here, you may be able to help the other secret agents."

Bart had put on the rubber suit and flippers. Now he hooked on the glass face mask.

"Come on," said Dan. "I'll carry the light. Keep close to me and I'll give you my breathing tube from time to time. We'll go up the anchor line to your boat. We'll go up slowly. But still, you will have to be put inside the decompression chamber."

"I'm ready," said Bart. "Before we start up, I want you to know one more important thing. I need your help in trapping the head of the smugglers."

"Who is he?" asked Dan.

"Jenkins," came the answer. "We have been after him for a long time. When he asked me to salvage the *Western Star*, I knew I had a good chance to trap him. Then when he told me about a secret black case he wanted and how he would give me a great deal if I got it, I knew I had him. I had to start trouble for you to make it look as if I really were on Jenkins' side."

Dan listened closely to Bart's story. As strange as it sounded, Dan did not think Bart was lying.

"Jenkins was against my coming down here to rescue you," Dan said. "He wants us to think you are the diamond smuggler."

"That sounds just like Jenkins," said Bart.

Dan looked at Bart. There was something about him he liked. "I'll help you in any way I can," he said.

Bart held out his hand. "Any man who would risk his life coming down here is just the man we need. Thank you, Dan," he said.

It had been a strange talk by two men who had been against one another on the surface. Now, twenty fathoms under the sea, they were working closely together. Dan shook Bart's hand. Then the two divers started out of the wreck.

Bart swam close to Dan. The underwater light Dan carried showed them the way through the dark ship. Now and then, Dan would take a deep breath through his breathing tube and then hand it to Bart. Bart would take a few breaths from the tube which came from Dan's air tanks and hand the tube back.

At last the two men were clear of the wreck. They swam to where the anchor line of the *Sea Devil* came down to the bottom. Bart put one hand on the line and slowly followed it up to the surface. Dan knew Bart must get into the decompression chamber soon to be sure he would not get the bends. If Bart had not been down so long, he could wait in the water for decompression to take place. But the water was too cold and the air in Dan's tanks might not last for the two men.

It was not long before the two men reached the surface of the water next to the *Sea Devil*. Dan signaled for help from several of the crew members who were on deck. They looked down in great surprise once they saw Bart with Dan. In a few minutes both divers were on deck. The crew of Bart's boat started asking many things, but Bart stopped them.

"We can talk about this after a while," he said. Then he put his hand on Dan's arm. "This man is not a killer. He just saved my life. I don't care what went on before, he's all right. Now get the decompression chamber ready for me. I was down there for too long a time."

Several of the crew opened the chamber which was lying on the deck. One man set the air gauge of the decompression chamber.

"Jenkins will be glad to know you are all right," the man said to Bart.

Bart was just about to enter the small chamber. He stopped and looked back.

"I want all of you to listen to this," he said. "No one away from this boat is to be told I'm up here. I have just found out that Jenkins is really working against all of us. I'll tell you more as soon as decompression is through."

With that, Bart closed the chamber and the air pressure inside started to rise. The crew of the ship turned to Dan.

"What's Bart talking about?" they asked.

Dan knew the crew did not know that Bart was a secret agent. He was not sure how much he could tell them.

"You will have to wait until Bart comes out," Dan said. "He can tell you the story. I have to get back to my boat."

Dan slipped over the side of the *Sea Devil* and swam for the *Sea Watch*. His crew had been watching for him and were waiting to pull him aboard. As Dan got out of the scuba gear, he told Carlos, Andy and Bill about finding Bart. He told them about bringing Bart up to the *Sea Devil* and seeing that he was put into the decompression chamber. Dan did not tell them that Bart was a secret agent.

"What did he say about the black case?" asked Carlos.

Dan did not want to keep anything from his crew. But he had told Bart he would not give away his secret.

"Bart may not be as wrong as we thought," Dan answered, after thinking for a minute. "It seems Jenkins sent him to get that case but never told him about any diamonds."

"Then Jenkins is the real smuggler," cried Bill.

"It looks that way," said Dan.

Andy shook his head up and down. "I have had a feeling that Jenkins was in back of this trouble all along," he said.

"Wait a minute, Dan," said Carlos. "If Bart is not in this with Jenkins, why did he attack you and cut his own suit?"

"I know that doesn't look good," said Dan. "Bart was working for Jenkins all right, but Jenkins is the head man."

The men sat and talked for a while. The sun was now high in the sky. A great deal had gone on that morning. Before long Jenkins rowed over alone from Mr. Duncan's boat. He smiled as he jumped aboard and walked over to where the men sat.

"Well," he said. "The Coast Guard will be here before night and this thing will be cleared up once and for all. I have the diamonds ready for them." Jenkins saw that the crew of the *Sea Watch* did not seem very glad to have him aboard.

"Look, men," he said. "Let's forget what went on before. You have the salvage job now. I'll be sure Mr. Duncan doesn't take it away this time. You wait and see."

"Thanks just the same, Jenkins," said Carlos, looking up with angry eyes. "But we don't need your help."

Jenkins moved in closer. "We have to work together," he said. "There is no telling what is going on over there." He pointed to the *Sea Devil*. "With Bart killed, his crew might attack our ships at any time. The other smugglers on his boat would attack now if they knew we had found the diamonds."

65

Then Jenkins reached into his jacket. "Look, I have brought guns for all of us just in case those smugglers try and start anything before the Coast Guard gets here."

He showed the guns to Dan. Dan waved them back with his hand.

"Listen, Jenkins," he said. "We have all the guns we need in case of an attack. You had better get back and stay with Mr. Duncan."

"But, Dan, I want to be your . . ." Jenkins started. But, as he said this, Salty, the parrot, flew down on top of his head.

"Help!" cried Jenkins, waving his arms. "Get away from here!" As he saw the men watching him, he tried to cover up how angry he was.

"That's some parrot you have there!" he smiled. "All right, Dan. I'll go back to Mr. Duncan if you say so. I was only trying to help you." He turned and walked to the side. In a few minutes he was on his way.

Dan watched Jenkins, the first mate of the *Western Star*. Then he looked over to the deck of the *Sea Devil*. Before long, Bart would be taken out of the decompression chamber. Once he was out, Dan knew it would be up to the two of them to set a trap for Jenkins, the diamond smuggler!

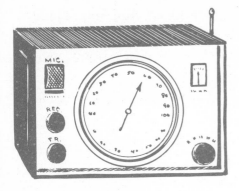

*Chapter Eight*

## THE GHOST

Dan waited until he knew Bart would be out of the decompression chamber. Then he got ready to row the small boat over to the *Sea Devil*.

"Why get into this any deeper, Dan?" asked Bill. "Bart and Jenkins are working together. They are both going to have to answer to the Coast Guard."

It was starting to get cold and Dan had just picked up a heavy jacket. As he put it on, he answered Bill. "I want to be sure Jenkins is trapped," he said. "There is a chance he might escape if Bart is left alone with his story. I know Bart is in this, too. But I want to see that Jenkins doesn't get away."

"That goes for me, too," said Andy. "I think Dan is right. I would like to go along to the *Sea Devil* and help."

Carlos and Bill said they wanted to stand by Dan, too. Dan told Bill to stay on the *Sea Watch* and guard the boat. Then Carlos, Andy and Dan got into the small boat and rowed to the *Sea Devil*. Bart had been taken from the decompression chamber and was lying down in his cabin. Carlos and Andy waited outside on the deck while Dan went in and talked to Bart alone.

"How are you feeling, Bart?" asked Dan as he opened the door and walked in. He sat down next to Bart.

"I'm in good shape, Dan," came the answer. "I'm sure I don't have the bends. Thank you again for your help."

"Forget it," said Dan. "What's next?"

Bart sat up and moved close to Dan. He talked in a whisper.

"Have you kept the secret I told you?" he asked.

"Yes," answered Dan.

"Good," said Bart. "I have a plan worked out. Have you seen Jenkins?"

Dan told him about Jenkins coming to the *Sea Watch*.

"Then he really thinks I lost my life in the *Western Star*," smiled Bart. "That's just what I hoped he would think." Bart took a small case from his jacket. "Do you see this, Dan?" he said. "This is a radio set."

Dan looked closely at the radio. It was so small it could be covered by a man's hand.

"With this radio I can send messages to the other secret agents near here," Bart went on. "Just before

68

you came I sent a message telling them to stand by until I call. They are with the Coast Guard, and can be here when we need them."

"What about you?" asked Dan. "Are you going to tell Jenkins and the others who you really are?"

"No, Dan," said Bart. "It is most important that no one find out. Now here is the plan."

Bart whispered his plan to Dan. In a while he got up and walked to a porthole. He looked out across the water. "The plan will work only after dark," he said. "It will be night very soon."

"What do your men know about all this?" asked Dan.

Bart walked back and sat down. "The men on this ship think Jenkins has called me a smuggler. They also think you and your men have come to help me get back at him." Then Bart held up the small radio set. "My men don't know that this set will be inside my diving helmet and sending messages to the agents while we trap Jenkins."

The two men talked for a while longer. Then Dan got up and went out on deck. He called Andy and Carlos and told them about Bart's plan.

"Do you really think this plan will trap Jenkins?" asked Carlos. "He may catch on to it."

Dan took a deep breath. "Yes, that's possible, Carlos," he said. "But I think the plan has a good chance of working."

"A ghost of a chance," said Andy. "Let's get Jenkins!"

"Get Jenkins!" cried Salty from Andy's shoulder. "Get Jenkins!"

Several of the crew members on Bart's ship heard Salty. They looked over and smiled. "That was some deal Jenkins tried to pull on Bart," one of them said. "But we'll take care of him."

The sun was starting to go down and soon Dan went back inside Bart's cabin.

"It will be dark in a while," he told Bart. "We are ready."

Bart walked to the porthole. "So am I," he said.

"We'll row over in our small boat," said Dan. "Jenkins is watching for a boat from your ship. He thinks your men are going to attack him. But he won't be upset if Carlos, Andy and I give him a call."

"Before we start out I must send a message," said Bart, picking up the small radio set. "Stand guard for me, Dan."

Dan stood by the porthole and listened for any sound from outside. Bart turned on the radio set. He held the radio close to his mouth and talked into it.

```
CALLING SEA SHARK FOUR, SEA SHARK FOUR.
THIS IS BLUE FISH ONE. BLUE FISH ONE
CALLING SEA SHARK FOUR. COME IN.
```

In a minute, Dan heard a voice coming from the set.

THIS IS SEA SHARK FOUR. WE HAVE YOU,
BLUE FISH ONE. GO AHEAD.

Bart talked into the set again.

BLUE FISH ONE IS READY WITH THE HOOK.
STAND BY FOR THE CATCH.

An answer came back right away.

WE HAVE YOU, BLUE FISH ONE. SEA SHARK
FOUR STANDING BY FOR THE CATCH. KEEP US
ON YOUR LINE. OVER AND OUT.

Dan had heard most of what was said. Now Dan
was sure Bart had not been lying. He was sure the
secret agents were about to close in and trap the head
of the diamond smugglers.

Before long, it was dark enough for the men to get
into the small boat. Bart had told his crew to wait
on the *Sea Devil*. Dan, Carlos and Andy got into the
small boat. Bart had put on a deep-sea diving suit.
He was carrying the helmet. He handed the helmet
down to Andy. Then he got into the small boat.

"All right," said Dan. "Let's go."

Dan and Carlos rowed the boat away from the *Sea Devil*. Just before they reached Mr. Duncan's boat, Andy covered the helmet on the bottom of the boat. Then he helped Bart into the water. Bart held on to the stern of the small boat. There were no stars glistening in the night sky. Bart could not be seen in the dark water. As they neared Mr. Duncan's boat, the men saw Jenkins come out on the deck holding a gun and a light.

"Who is there?" he called. "Who is out there?"

"Take it easy, Jenkins," called Dan. "We have come to talk with you."

"Is that you, Dan?" said Jenkins, looking out over the dark water. "Come on aboard."

The men saw Mr. Duncan and two other men come out on deck.

"Keep down," Dan whispered to Bart as they pulled up next to the ship.

Jenkins reached down to help the men aboard. "Glad you came over," he said.

"I am coming aboard for only a minute," said Dan. "Carlos and Andy will wait in the boat. I want to show you my plan for starting the salvage work."

With that, Dan went aboard. He walked away with Jenkins and Mr. Duncan and the two men. When they were gone, Carlos and Andy helped Bart up out of the water. No one was on deck. The two men took Bart to the dark shadows where he could not be seen. Then they brought up the helmet and helped Bart put it on.

"You're on your own," whispered Carlos.

"So far, so good," Bart answered. The faceplate in his helmet had been taken off so that he could be heard.

Andy and Carlos got back into the small boat. Soon Dan, Mr. Duncan and Jenkins walked out on deck.

"I think your plan with the floating docks is a good one," Mr. Duncan was saying. "We can send to shore for the docks in the morning."

"I'm all for it, too," said Jenkins. He put his hand on Dan's shoulder. "Glad to be working with you."

Dan smiled and walked away. He jumped down into the small boat.

"Bart is all set," whispered Carlos as Dan took his place by an oar.

Dan and Carlos rowed away from the ship into the dark. Then they stopped. They saw Jenkins go into his cabin.

"We'll wait a few minutes, then go back," said Dan.

Jenkins had been in his cabin only a few minutes when he heard several knocks on the door.

"Who—who is there?" called Jenkins. "Who is that knocking out there?"

There was no answer.

Jenkins picked up a gun. Then he opened the cabin door and looked out into the dark shadows.

"What the . . ." Jenkins started. He dropped the gun and fell back from the door. He looked as if he had seen a ghost. There stood Bart. Water ran down from his diving suit and he had a cold, angry look in his eyes. Slowly Bart walked in and closed the cabin door.

"Where did you come from?" cried Jenkins in a shaking voice. "I—I thought you were trapped. What —what do you want?"

Bart stopped and pointed at Jenkins.

"I have come up from the *Western Star* to get you," he said. "You ran out on me, Jenkins. You wanted me left down there."

"No!" cried Jenkins. "You're wrong! I'm glad you're here, Bart. Don't worry. I will make this all up to you."

By now Jenkins had pulled himself together. He looked down at the gun he had dropped. Bart saw that Jenkins was looking at the gun. He started moving closer to Jenkins. As Jenkins made a move to reach for it, Bart knocked the gun across the cabin. He moved toward Jenkins, holding up a hand as if to hit him.

"Help! Help!" cried Jenkins, moving back. "Listen, Bart. Those were diamonds in that case. I will give you some of them. The Coast Guard is coming, but I'm

the only one who knows how many diamonds were in
the case. I have taken some out and you can have them.
If you work with me, the other smugglers will make it
worth your while. There are many more diamonds to
bring in. I have many smugglers working for me. They
will never catch us."

"Don't be so sure, Jenkins," said Dan, walking in
and holding a gun on the surprised first mate. Mr.
Duncan, Carlos and Andy were behind Dan. They had
all been listening. What they did not know was that
the other secret agents had been listening, too, by
means of the small radio set in Bart's helmet.

Jenkins pointed at Bart and cried out, "He's the
one! He's the one! You're all wrong. I'm not a smuggler.
Bart is the one."

Bart looked at Jenkins. "I know I was pulled into
this by you," he said. "And I'm ready to face what's
coming to me. But your days as head of the smugglers
are over."

Mr. Duncan moved toward Jenkins.

"To think how I let you use me," he said.

"They are all wrong," cried Jenkins. "It's Bart the
Coast Guard is after!"

"We'll see," said Dan.

Before long, the Coast Guard ship was there. The
secret agents came aboard and took both Bart and
Jenkins away with them. As he was being taken away,

Bart looked over at Dan for a minute. The two men did not say anything, but Dan knew what Bart was thinking. "Don't worry," thought Dan. "I'll keep your secret." He wanted to tell Bart what a good job he had done, but he did not. He just smiled in a knowing way as Bart went by under the guard of the secret agents.

Then Dan turned and went back to where Mr. Duncan, Carlos and Andy were standing. Dan and the crew of the *Sea Watch* were ready to start with the salvage of the wreck of the *Western Star*.

# EXERCISES

## Chapter One

# TWENTY FATHOMS DOWN

*Choose the right word or words for these sentences.*

1. Dan was the owner of the *Sea Watch*. He was also
    a) a deep-sea diver.
    b) a cook.
    c) the owner of the motors.

2. Mr. Duncan was the owner of
    a) the *Sea Watch*.
    b) an underwater mountain.
    c) the *Western Star*.

3. Jenkins was
    a) a crew member of the *Sea Watch*.
    b) a deep-sea diver.
    c) first mate of the *Western Star*.

4. Carlos was
    a) first mate of the *Western Star*.
    b) Dan's first mate.
    c) a parrot.

5. Bill was
    a) a crew member who ran the *Sea Watch*.
    b) a crew member of the *Western Star*.
    c) a deep-sea diver.

6. The *Western Star* was lying on
   a) the side of an underwater mountain.
   b) the shore.
   c) the surface of the water.


7. The *Western Star* had gone down in
   a) twenty feet of mud.
   b) twenty fathoms of water.
   c) two fathoms of water.


8. Mr. Duncan wanted Dan and his crew to bring up
   a) the cargo from the *Sea Watch*.
   b) the great gray ghost.
   c) the cargo from the *Western Star*.


9. The *Western Star* was carrying a cargo of
   a) several hundred motors.
   b) twenty telephones.
   c) several hundred fish.


10. Dan could see there would be only one way to salvage the cargo. They would have to send for
    a) an air hose and line.
    b) two floating docks.
    c) the crew of the *Western Star*.

## Chapter Two

# THE SEA DEVIL

*Choose the right word or words for these sentences.*

1.  The wreck was slipping
    a) down the mountain.
    b) on the shore.
    c) on the cables.

2.  Dan could not move very quickly because
    a) the fish shot by him.
    b) his deep-sea diving gear was too heavy.
    c) his shoulder was hurt.

3.  Dan talked to Bill on the telephone from
    a) the bottom of the sea.
    b) inside the wreck.
    c) the deck of the *Sea Devil.*

4.  Dan was pulled up slowly so that he would not get
    a) the cargo.
    b) the bends.
    c) surprised.

5.  Dan told Mr. Duncan,
    a) "We will need two floating docks."
    b) "You can clear out of here fast."
    c) "Ship ahoy! Ship ahoy!"

6. Jenkins told Mr. Duncan that to send for floating docks
    a) would take a long time.
    b) would not take a long time.
    c) would not damage the cargo.

7. The owner of the *Sea Devil* was
    a) Andy.
    b) Carlos.
    c) Bart.

8. Jenkins said that Bart and his crew would not
    a) be afraid to go after the cargo in the holds.
    b) be afraid of the mud.
    c) be able to bring up the cargo.

9. One of the men of the *Sea Devil* rowed to the *Sea Watch* and asked
    a) Carlos for a telephone.
    b) Dan to go down and see what was wrong.
    c) Bill to help Dan into his diving gear.

10. Down on the bottom of the sea, Dan saw that Bart had gone
    a) inside the air hose.
    b) inside the wreck.
    c) around the *Sea Devil*.

*Chapter Three*

# KNIFE ATTACK!

*Choose the right word or words for these sentences.*

1. On all sides of the hold Dan could see
   a) hundreds of hammers.
   b) several diving helmets.
   c) hundreds of cases of motors.

2. In one of the holds, Dan found he was standing
   a) in mud.
   b) in an air lock.
   c) on some motor cases.

3. The air Dan found himself standing in was
   a) trapped air.
   b) air that had escaped through portholes.
   c) air from Bart's air hose.

4. Dan found Bart trying to hammer
   a) an opening in the hold.
   b) open one of the cases.
   c) open a porthole.

5. As Bart moved slowly toward him, Dan reached
   a) for the telephone.
   b) for the hammer.
   c) for the knife which was hooked at his side.

6. When Dan stopped to look back at the wreck,
    a) a big fish knocked him down.
    b) his air hose started slipping.
    c) Bart grabbed him.

7. Bart took Dan's knife and cut
    a) Dan's shoulder.
    b) Dan's suit.
    c) his own suit.

8. Bart pulled four times on his line. This was a signal
    a) to pull him up very fast.
    b) to send down more air.
    c) to send down the decompression chamber.

9. Dan called over the telephone to Bill. He said,
    a) "There is an air lock down here."
    b) "Something very strange has taken place."
    c) "The air lock needs more air."

10. Bart told Mr. Duncan that
    a) Dan tried to kill him.
    b) Dan needed help.
    c) Dan slipped down the mountain.

*Chapter Four*

# BART'S STORY

*Choose the right word or words for these sentences.*

1. Carlos and Bill helped Dan
    a) find his knife.
    b) pull up his air hose.
    c) take off his diving suit.

2. Andy said he had a cooking knife or two that would
    a) cut up Bart's suit.
    b) cut up a big fish.
    c) open a motor case.

3. Carlos said it sounded as if Bart was
    a) diving in the decompression chamber.
    b) after something inside the hold.
    c) trying to help bring up the cargo.

4. Mr. Duncan and Jenkins were waiting for Bart
    a) to come up from the bottom.
    b) to go into the hold.
    c) to come out of the decompression chamber.

5. Mr. Duncan told Jenkins, "I don't think Dan
    a) would ever try to kill any one."
    b) wants the salvage job."
    c) will do anything to escape."

6. Dan and Carlos rowed a small boat over to
   a) Mr. Duncan's ship.
   b) the *Sea Devil*.
   c) the *Sea Watch*.

7. The men on the *Sea Devil* were waiting for Carlos when
   a) he jumped aboard, ready to fight.
   b) he tried to call Dan on the telephone.
   c) he tried to open a case of motors.

8. The man who pulled the crew members away from Carlos was
   a) Mr. Duncan.
   b) Andy.
   c) Jenkins.

9. Jenkins made Mr. Duncan think that
   a) Dan tried to kill Bart.
   b) Dan tried to help Bart.
   c) Dan tried to telephone Bart.

10. Mr. Duncan turned the salvage job over to
   a) the Coast Guard.
   b) Bart.
   c) Jenkins.

## Chapter Five

# TRAPPED!

*Choose the right word or words for these sentences.*

1. Salty flew across the water to the
   a) shore.
   b) deck of the *Sea Devil.*
   c) deck of the *Western Star.*

2. Andy had trouble rowing the boat because
   a) he had never done much rowing before.
   b) it was too big for one man to row.
   c) he was afraid of Jenkins.

3. When Andy called, "Come on, Salty," the parrot
   a) came to him.
   b) flew to the *Sea Watch.*
   c) flew away.

4. When Jenkins grabbed for the parrot, he
   a) hit the deck.
   b) fell head first into the water.
   c) smiled at Andy.

5. Jenkins said,
   a) "Good for Salty."
   b) "Stay on the *Sea Watch* after this."
   c) "I'll get you for this."

6. As Bart worked to open case 749, Carlos watched him from
   a) the deck of the *Sea Watch*.
   b) a small boat.
   c) inside the wreck.

7. Bart opened case 749 and
   a) pulled out a good, new motor.
   b) put a secret message inside the motor.
   c) brought out a small, black case.

8. As the two divers were readying for a fight,
   a) the wreck started slipping.
   b) Bart dropped his knife.
   c) the air in the air lock ran out.

9. Carlos grabbed the small, black case and
   a) put it back in case 749.
   b) swam fast for open water.
   c) opened it before Bart could get up.

10. Deep inside the *Western Star* Bart had not moved from the hold.
    a) He was waiting for Carlos to open the case.
    b) He was trapped under the sea.
    c) He was putting on his faceplate.

*Chapter Six*

# THE BLACK CASE

*Choose the right word or words for these sentences.*

1. Back on the *Sea Watch,* Carlos told the men
    a) how he had taken the black case from Bart.
    b) to go back and get Bart.
    c) to show him the diamonds.

2. Mr. Duncan came to the *Sea Watch* to ask
    a) the crew to go away.
    b) Dan to see if he could save Bart.
    c) Andy to keep his parrot away from Jenkins.

3. Dan and Carlos showed Mr. Duncan
    a) Andy's parrot.
    b) the black case.
    c) the scuba gear.

4. Inside the black case, Mr. Duncan found
    a) secret messages.
    b) many diamonds.
    c) a motor.

5. Mr. Duncan said,
    a) "This is the work of smugglers."
    b) "This case must be put back on the wreck."
    c) "This case is part of my cargo."

6. Mr. Duncan wanted to
    a) give the black case to Dan.
    b) radio the Coast Guard and give them the diamonds.
    c) keep the diamonds.

7. Jenkins said,
    a) "I think Dan should dive down and get Bart."
    b) "I will send my divers down to rescue Bart."
    c) "I would not want Dan to risk his life for that smuggler."

8. Mr. Duncan handed the black case to
    a) Jenkins.
    b) Dan.
    c) Carlos.

9. Dan got ready to dive down to
    a) look for more diamonds.
    b) try to save the motors.
    c) try to rescue Bart.

10. Just before he dived, Dan asked for
    a) an air hose and rope.
    b) a rubber suit, flippers, and face mask.
    c) a set of hammers.

## Chapter Seven

# BART'S SECRET

*Choose the right word or words for these sentences.*

1. When Dan found Bart he said,
    a) "Bart, I have come to help you."
    b) "Bart, give up now."
    c) "Are there any more diamonds here?"

2. Dan told Bart that Mr. Duncan
    a) was a smuggler.
    b) had the diamonds now.
    c) would not let him do any more salvage work.

3. Bart said to Dan,
    a) "Keep away from me."
    b) "I am a secret agent."
    c) "I want to salvage the *Western Star*."

4. Bart told Dan that the head of the smugglers was
    a) Jenkins.
    b) Andy.
    c) Mr. Duncan.

5. Bart told his crew
    a) that he was a secret agent.
    b) to get the decompression chamber ready.
    c) to get Dan.

6. Bart told his crew,
   a) "No one away from this boat is to be told I'm up here."
   b) "Tell Mr. Duncan that I have been rescued."
   c) "Carlos has the diamonds."

7. When Dan got back to the *Sea Watch*, he
   a) told the men Bart was a secret agent.
   b) told the men Jenkins was the head of the smugglers.
   c) did not tell the men Jenkins was the head of the smugglers.

8. Jenkins wanted to give the crew of the *Sea Watch*
   a) diamonds.
   b) guns.
   c) motors.

9. When Salty flew at him, Jenkins was
   a) angry.
   b) glad.
   c) afraid.

10. It was up to Dan and Bart to
    a) fight each other.
    b) set a trap for Jenkins.
    c) call for help.

## Chapter Eight

# THE GHOST

*Choose the right word or words for these sentences.*

1. Dan wanted to be sure that
   a) Mr. Duncan escaped.
   b) the diamonds were saved.
   c) Jenkins was trapped.

2. Bart told Dan he would use
   a) a radio set inside his diving helmet.
   b) a rope to tie up Jenkins.
   c) an air hose to help him stay under water.

3. Dan knew Bart had not been lying because
   a) he saw him give Carlos the diamonds.
   b) he heard him talk to the agents in code.
   c) Jenkins said so.

4. The men who went with Bart to trap Jenkins were
   a) secret agents.
   b) Dan, Carlos and Andy.
   c) Dan, Bill and Mr. Duncan.

5. Jenkins tried to give Bart
   a) many salvage jobs.
   b) help to get away from the Coast Guard.
   c) some of the diamonds.

6. Dan and Mr. Duncan knew Jenkins was a smuggler because
   a) they had heard what he had said to Bart.
   b) they found the diamonds on him.
   c) the Coast Guard told them about it.

7. Jenkins said that the Coast Guard was really after
   a) Bart.
   b) Mr. Duncan.
   c) the crew of the *Sea Devil*.

8. The Coast Guard came and took
   a) Mr. Duncan and Dan.
   b) Jenkins and Bart.
   c) the crew of the *Sea Devil*.

9. Dan
   a) told Carlos that Bart was a secret agent.
   b) kept Bart's secret.
   c) told Andy that Bart was in the Coast Guard.

10. Dan and the crew of the *Sea Watch* were ready to
    a) go to shore.
    b) go and see the crew of the *Sea Devil*.
    c) start with the salvage of the *Western Star*.

# VOCABULARY

*Danger Below,* the sixth book in the *Deep-Sea Adventure Series,* uses a vocabulary of 455 different words for a total of 12,936 running words. All but 60 words, which are italicized in the list below, may be considered basic vocabulary words. *Danger Below* repeats 388 words from the first five books of the series, *The Sea Hunt, Treasure under the Sea, Submarine Rescue, The Pearl Divers,* and *Frogmen in Action,* while adding 67 new ones.

| | | | | |
|---|---|---|---|---|
| a | before | Coast Guard | ever | guard |
| able | began | cold | eyes | gun |
| *aboard* | behind | come | | |
| about | below | cook | face | had |
| across | bends | could | *faceplate* | hammer |
| afraid | better | cover | far | hand |
| after | big | *crew* | fast | has |
| again | Bill | cried | *fathoms* | have |
| against | black | cut | feel | he |
| *agent* | *blood* | | feet | head |
| ahead | blue | *damaged* | fell | hear |
| *ahoy* | boat | Dan | few | heard |
| air | both | danger | fight | heavy |
| all | bottom | dark | find | held |
| almost | bow | day | first | *helmet* |
| alone | breath | *deal* | fish | help |
| along | breathe | *deck* | flew | here |
| also | bring | *decompression* | *flippers* | *he's* |
| am | brought | deep | floated | high |
| an | bubbles | deeper | followed | him |
| *anchor* | but | deep-sea | for | himself |
| and | by | Devil | forget | his |
| Andy | | diamond | found | hit |
| angry | cabin | did | four | hold |
| another | *cable* | didn't | from | *hook* |
| answer | call | distance | full | hope |
| any | came | *dive* | | hose |
| anything | can | *diver* | *gauge* | how |
| are | can't | do | *gear* | hundred |
| arm | care | *docks* | get | hurt |
| around | *cargo* | *doesn't* | *ghost* | |
| as | Carlos | done | give | I |
| ask | carry | don't | glad | if |
| at | case | door | glass | I'll |
| *attack* | catch | down | *glistened* | I'm |
| away | *chamber* | drops | go | *important* |
| | chance | Duncan | gone | in |
| back | change | | good | inside |
| Bart | clear | easy | got | into |
| be | close | enough | *grab* | is |
| because | closely | *enter* | gray | it |
| been | closer | *escape* | great | it's |

96

jacket
Jenkins
*job*
jump
just

keep
kept
kill
*killer*
knew
knife
knock
know

last
laughed
left
let
let's
life
light
like
line
listen
lock
long
longer
look
lost
lying

made
make
man
many
*mask*
*mate*
may
me
mean
*member*
men
*message*
might
mind
minute
*mission*
more
morning
most
*motor*
mountain
mouth

move
Mr.
much
mud
must
my

near
need
never
next
night
no
not
now

*oar*
of
off
on
once
one
only
open
or
other
our
out
outside
over
own
*owner*

*parrot*
part
picked
place
plan
point
*porthole*
*possible*
*pressure*
pull
*pump*
put

quickly

radio
ran
reach
ready
real
really

*rescue*
right
rise
*risk*
rock
row
rubber

said
Salty
*salvage*
same
sat
save
saw
say
*scuba*
sea
secret
see
seem
seen
send
sent
set
several
shadows
shaking
shape
*shark*
ship
shook
shore
shot
should
shoulder
show
side
signal
*skipper*
sky
slip
slowly
small
smiles
*smuggler*
so
some
something
soon
sound
splash
squeezed
stand

stars
start
stay
*stern*
still
stood
stop
story
strange
suit
sun
sure
*surface*
surprise
swam

take
taken
talk
*tanks*
telephone
tell
thank
that
that's
the
their
them
then
there
these
they
thing
think
this
those
thought
through
tied
tightly
time
to
together
told
too
took
top
toward
trap
trouble
try
*tube*
turn

twenty
two

under
*underwater*
until
up
upset
us
use

very
voice

wait
walked
want
was
watch
water
waved
way
we
wear
well
we'll
went
were
Western
what
what's
when
where
which
while
whisper
who
why
will
with
won't
work
worry
worth
would
*wreck*
wrong

yes
you
your
you're